# GRANDPA GREEN

LANE SMITH

First published in the USA 2011 by Roaring Brook Press
This edition published 2017 by Two Hoots
an imprint of Pan Macmillan
20 New Wharf Road, London N1 9RR
Associated companies throughout the world
www.panmacmillan.com
ISBN: 978-1-4472-1835-7

Book design by Molly Leach


9 8 7 6 5 4 3 2 1
A CIP catalogue record for this book is available from the British Library.
Printed in China

The characters in this book were rendered with brush and waterproof drawing ink. The foliage was created with watercolour, oil paint and digital paint.

www.twohootsbooks.com

He was born a really long time ago,

before computers or mobile phones or television.

He grew up on a farm with
pigs and corn and carrots . . .

and eggs.

In nursery school
he got chicken pox.*

*Not from the chickens.

He had to stay home from school.
So he read stories about secret gardens
and wizards and a little engine that could.

In junior school
he stole his first kiss.

After senior school his wish was to study horticulture,

but he went to a world war instead.

He met his future
wife in a little café.

When the war was over, they were married.

They had many happy years
together and never, ever fought.

At least to hear *him* tell it.

They had children, lots more grandchildren,
and a great-grandchild, me.

He used to remember everything.

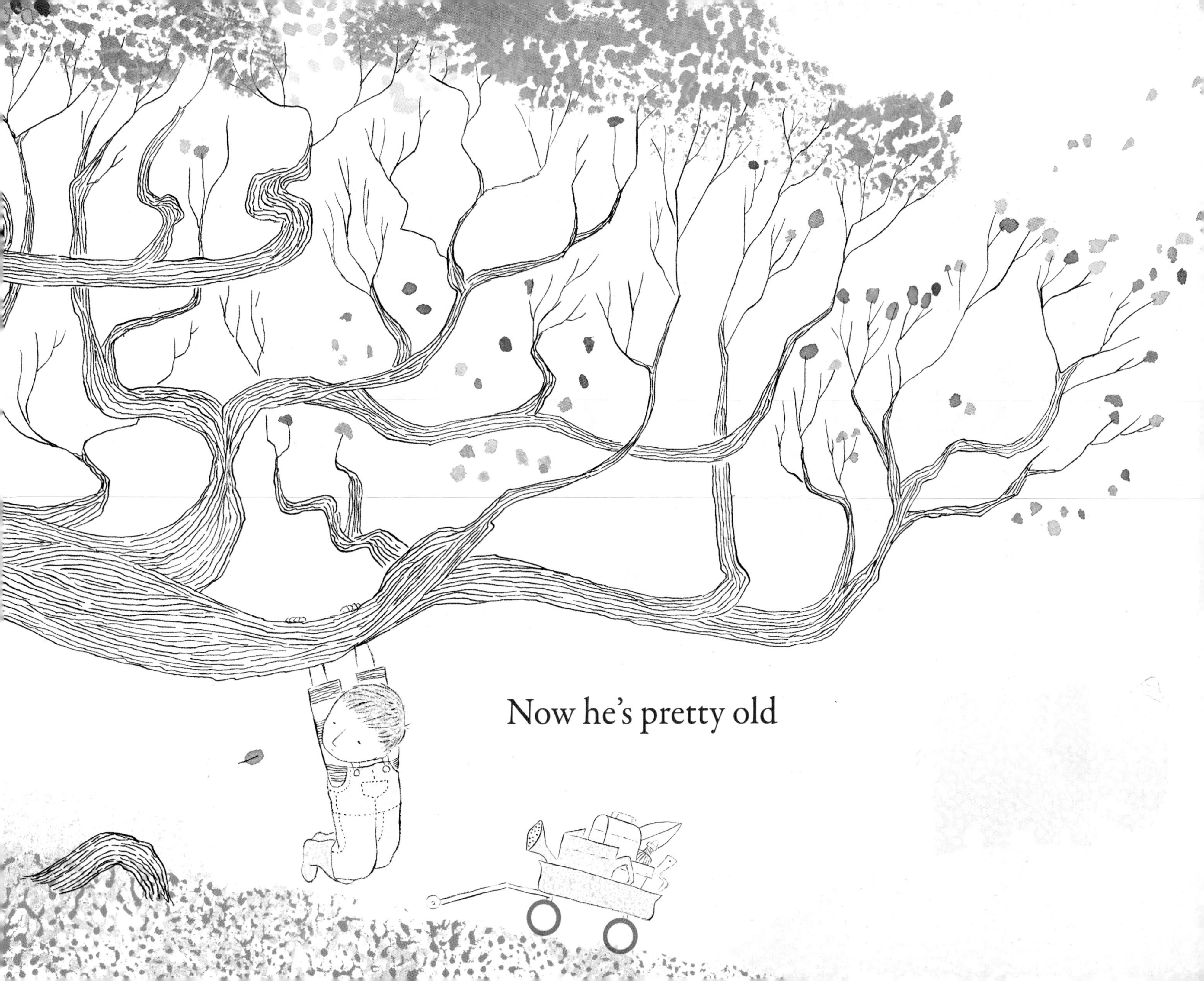

Now he's pretty old

and he sometimes forgets things

like his favourite floppy straw hat.

But the important stuff,

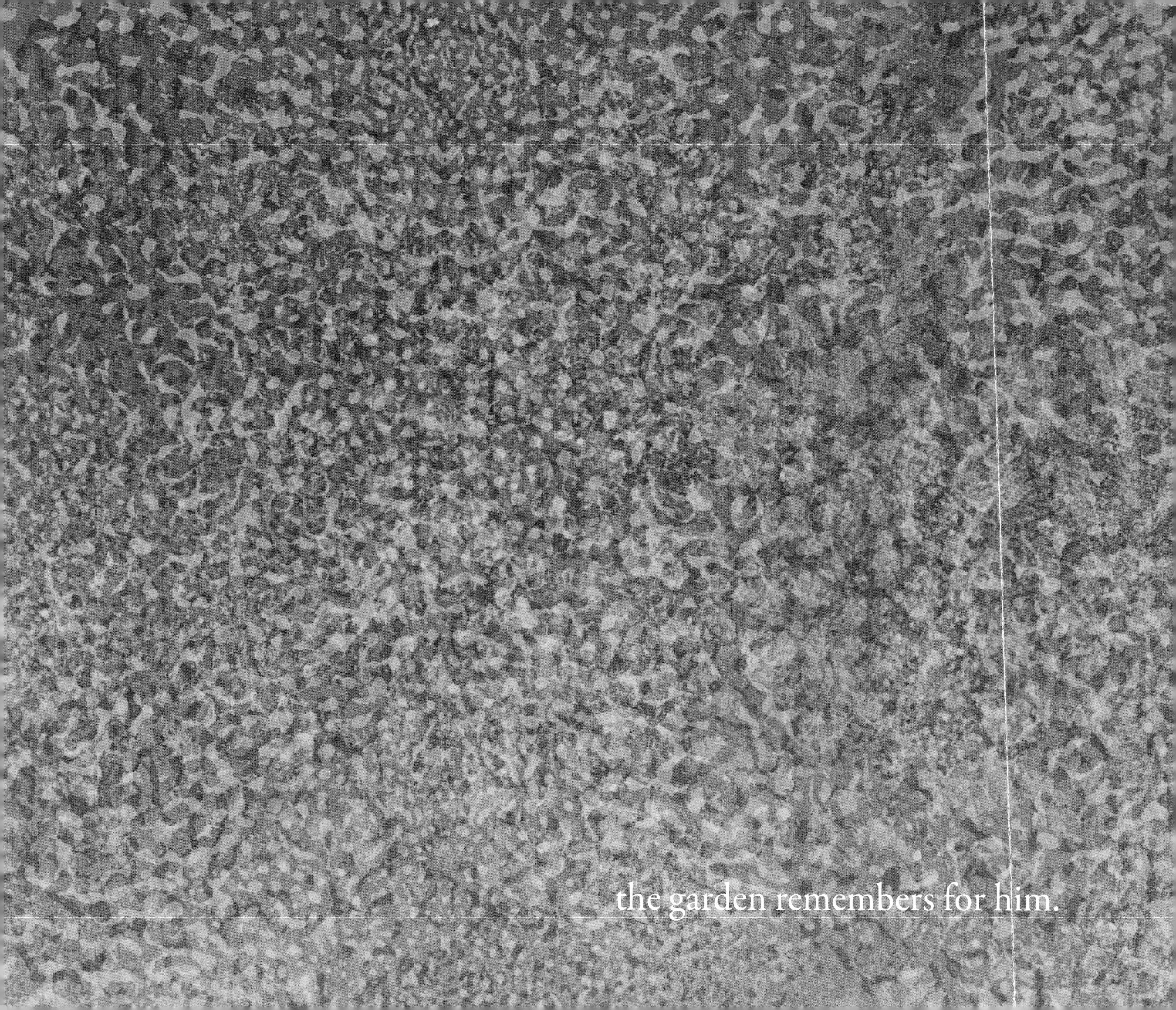
the garden remembers for him.